P9-CFS-500

THE BOY THOU

A LAURA GERINGER BOOK

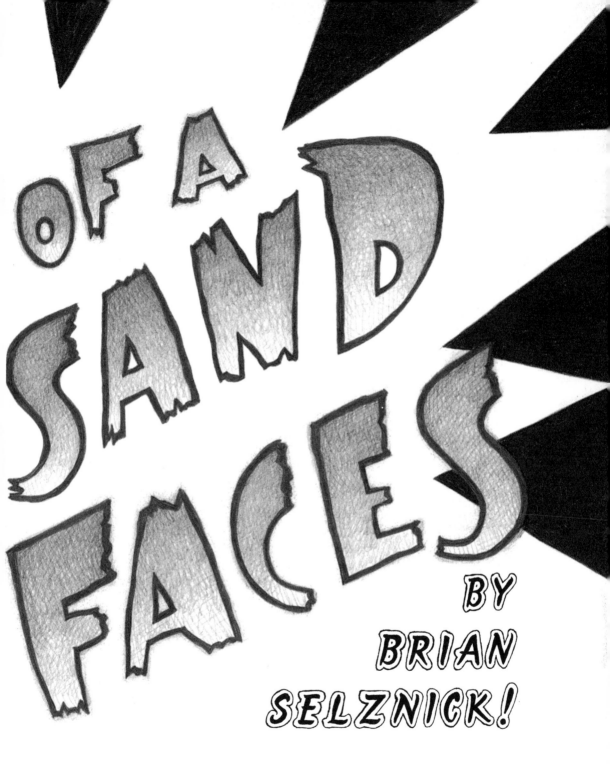

OF A SAND FACES

BY BRIAN SELZNICK!

AN IMPRINT OF HARPERCOLLINSPUBLISHERS

Library of Congress Cataloging-in-Publication Data Selznick, Brian.   The boy of a thousand faces /
by Brian Selznick.   p.   cm.   Summary: Obsessed with horror films, ten-year-old Alonzo dreams of
transforming himself into "The Boy of a Thousand Faces" and gets his wish in an unexpected way.
ISBN 0-06-026265-6. — ISBN 0-06-026266-4 (lib. bdg.)   [1. Horror films—Fiction.   2. Monsters—
Fiction.   3. Halloween—Fiction.]   I. Title. PZ7.S4654Bo 2000 99-47352 [Fic]—dc21   CIP   AC
Typography by Alicia Mikles 1   2   3   4   5   6   7   8   9   10 ❖ First Edition

For Chris Krovatin (a real Boy of a Thousand Faces)
and everyone else who loves monsters.

Special thanks to Clark Fleury, Gregory Battaglia, Holly Fritzky
and her Students, and the Capitol Hill Day School.

We hereby acknowledge the following:
Page 2: Patterson/Gimlin © Rene Dahinden, 1967. Page 3: © Fortean Picture Library.
Page 10: © 2001 by Universal City Studios, Inc.; courtesy of Universal Studios Publishing Rights, and also
Chaney Enterprises. All rights reserved. Front and back endpapers: stamp designs © 1996 U.S. Postal Service.
™ & © collectively: Chaney Enterprises, Lugosi Enterprises,
Karloff Enterprises and Universal Studios, Inc. All rights reserved.

After the Crowd

lit their torches

and chased the phantom

into the river,

after the hunchback

met his death

in the darkness of the tower,

and after the creature

disappeared back

into its black lagoon,

Alonzo King went to bed.

MY LIFE AT TEN was a black-and-white horror movie, and I was the star. I lived in a haunted house with a secret graveyard out back and an ancient city buried beneath the basement. Little people, no bigger than my thumbs, lived under the floorboards in my room. Ghosts hovered over my shoulders, and aliens waited to do terrible experiments in the dark of night. Books with titles like *The Lost City of Atlantis* and *Stories of Strange Disappearances* lined the bookshelves of my room. I swam with the Loch Ness monster and ran with Big Foot. I believed in the unbelievable and collected whatever proof I could find.

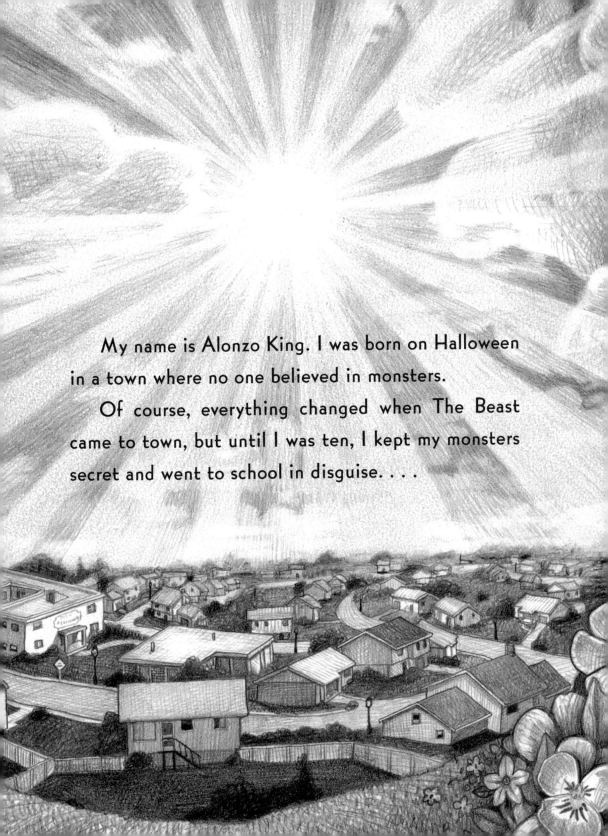

My name is Alonzo King. I was born on Halloween in a town where no one believed in monsters.

Of course, everything changed when The Beast came to town, but until I was ten, I kept my monsters secret and went to school in disguise. . . .

Who would have thought that the quiet boy in the corner was capable, at any moment, of exploding into a six-armed, slime-covered creature from another planet? Who would have thought that the only boy not playing soccer during gym class had seen ghosts and communicated with the dead? Who would have thought that same boy could name every monster movie ever made and tell you how to bring a corpse back to life? Who would have thought it? No one.

Well, no one except Mr. Shadows.

MONSTERS at MIDNIGHT

WITH YOUR HOST
MR. SHADOWS

Mr. Shadows was the host of a late-night horror show called *Monsters at Midnight*, on Channel 37, and he was my hero.

Mr. Shadows wore a white mask and a black cape and began each show by saying, "Welcome to *Monsters at Midnight*. I am your host, Mr. Shadows." My mom didn't want me watching his show because sometimes it gave me nightmares, but where else could I have seen movies like *Frankenstein*, *Dracula*, *The Wolf Man*, *The Bride of Frankenstein*, *Attack of the Fifty Foot Woman*, *The Incredible Shrinking Man*, and of course my favorite, *The Phantom of the Opera*?

I had seen the movie dozens of times. The Phantom was played by an incredible actor named Lon Chaney, who was called "The Man of a Thousand Faces." He died in 1930, and no one ever knew what he *really* looked like because in one movie he might be a vampire with a row of sharp white fangs, and then in another he might be a hunchback, or a Chinese grandfather, or a little old lady, or a legless criminal. He might be blind or bald or covered in hair, and people joked with each other not to step on spiders, because you never knew. . . it might be Lon Chaney.

More than anything, I wanted to be The Boy of a Thousand Faces. Alone in my room I would transform my face with paint and makeup and tape. Then I would borrow my mom's old Polaroid camera, take pictures of myself, and put them in a special notebook that no one knew about. So far there were only twenty-three Polaroids of me in monster makeup, but a *thousand* was my goal. I had a long way to go.

I thought I would never get there, until one quiet morning as I was heading out to school, my friend Mr. Blake opened his door and called me over.

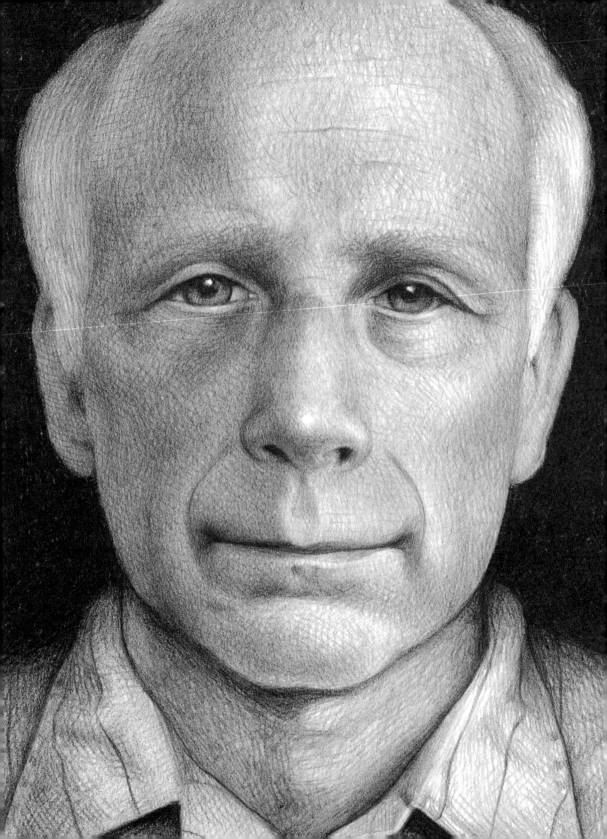

Mr. Blake was the local postman, and he lived with his old dog, Gaston, in the apartment down the hall from mine. I loved listening to his stories and looking through his mysterious collections. He had fossils and glass animals and windup toys, and he always told me that in a box somewhere he owned George Washington's baby teeth and Amelia Earhart's goggles. I could never tell if he was joking.

Mr. Blake also gave me new stamps whenever they came out, and sure enough, that morning he handed me a little booklet. "Wow!" was all I could say when I saw them. These were even better than the dinosaur stamps he had given me once. These were *monster* stamps, and they immediately gave me an idea! After school that day I tore a blank sheet of paper out of my notebook and began to write. . . .

Dear Mr. Shadows,

I want to be the boy of a thousand faces but so far I only have 23. Can you help me? This photograph is the scariest face I ever made ~ and I wanted you to see it. I live in a town ~ where no one believes in monsters. I love your show. My favorite movie is The Phantom of the Opera. My birthday is on Halloween.

Your friend,
Alonzo King age 10

P.S. Do you think I will ever be the boy of a thousand faces?

32 USA

Lon Chaney as
The PHANTOM
OPERA

I carefully placed a Phantom of the Opera stamp in the corner of an envelope. Then I removed the scariest face I had ever made from my notebook and mailed everything to Mr. Shadows at *Monsters at Midnight*. The next morning I ran off to school, full of expectations. But in the next few weeks I forgot all about that letter . . . because The Beast came to town.

Stories began to spread that something strange was lurking in our town, and people named it The Beast! Kids who had always laughed at me when I talked about monsters were suddenly whispering about The Beast between classes. Even my mom asked me about it. I realized this was my big chance! After all, I was the only person in town who knew anything at all about monsters.

I became an expert on The Beast. I knew who had discovered that their gladiolas had been crushed in the night and who had noticed what looked like claw prints on the side of their new car. I walked through the halls of school and heard the other kids say, "Ask Alonzo—he'll know."

I had never been happier in my life. Soon The Beast was the only thing anyone talked about. I forgot all about becoming The Boy of a Thousand Faces. The only thing I wanted was to see The Beast for myself.

As the weeks passed, jack-o'-lanterns began to appear on all the porches around town, and paper ghosts filled the trees. People usually ignored Halloween, but this year was different. I barely noticed, though, because I was busy tracking down The Beast. Mr. Blake was as interested in the monster as I was, and when he came home from the post office, we both got goose bumps as we told one another what we had heard about The Beast.

Soon it was the morning before Halloween. I opened the paper as I ate my breakfast and saw a giant headline that read, "Is This The Beast?" Someone had sent in a photograph of The Beast!

There, in black and white, was the photograph I
had sent to Mr. Shadows of myself in monster makeup!
The Beast that I had longed to find . . . was me!

I ran to the phone and called Channel 37. I asked to speak to Mr. Shadows, saying it was an emergency, but the man on the other end just laughed. He said Mr. Shadows had *died* years ago, and all of his shows were repeats! "That's impossible," I screamed, but I heard a click and the line went dead.

I headed out to school. People were putting up the last of their Halloween decorations, and I heard everyone talking about The Beast. A few had even ripped out the blurry photo from the paper. I suddenly began to yell, "Stop it! It's me! I'm The Beast. . . . It's all a mistake—there is no Beast!"

No one listened to me at all.

So Halloween came, and my mother gave me orange cupcakes to take to school. As I passed Mr. Blake's apartment door, it opened and he wished me a happy birthday. He said he had a couple of presents for me and invited me inside.

I figured he had some more stamps for me, but he said, "This is for you, Alonzo. Be very careful—it's an actual paw print of The Beast! Very rare." I thought he was kidding, but Mr. Blake handed me something golden, and smiled.

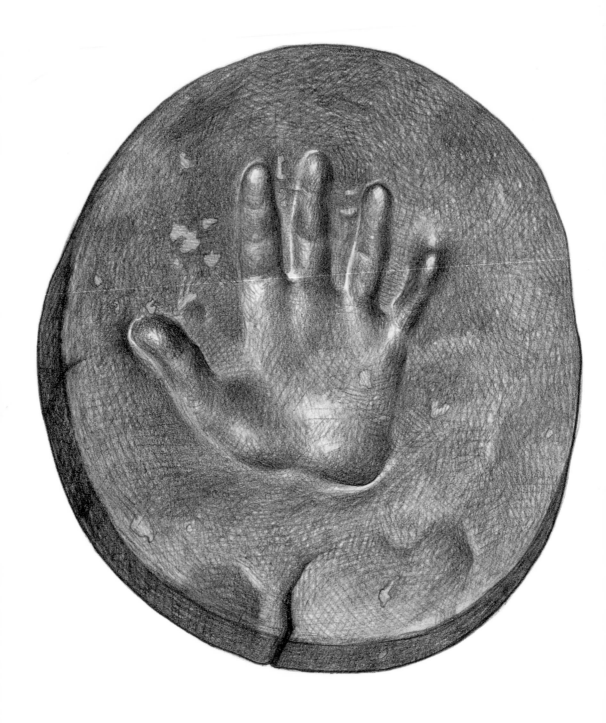

It was a child's handprint, set in plaster, that had been spray painted gold. Written on the back were the words "Alonzo King, Age 4." I didn't understand.

"Don't you remember giving that to me when you were little?" Mr. Blake said. "You used to come over and play with Gaston all the time, and I'd baby-sit you when your mom was away. Once I even showed you my favorite movie, *The Phantom of the Opera*."

Then he said, "Let me give you your second present. . . . " He handed me a small wrapped package. Inside was an old white mask, which Mr. Blake held up to his face. "Welcome to *Monsters at Midnight*," he said. "I am your host, Mr. Shadows."

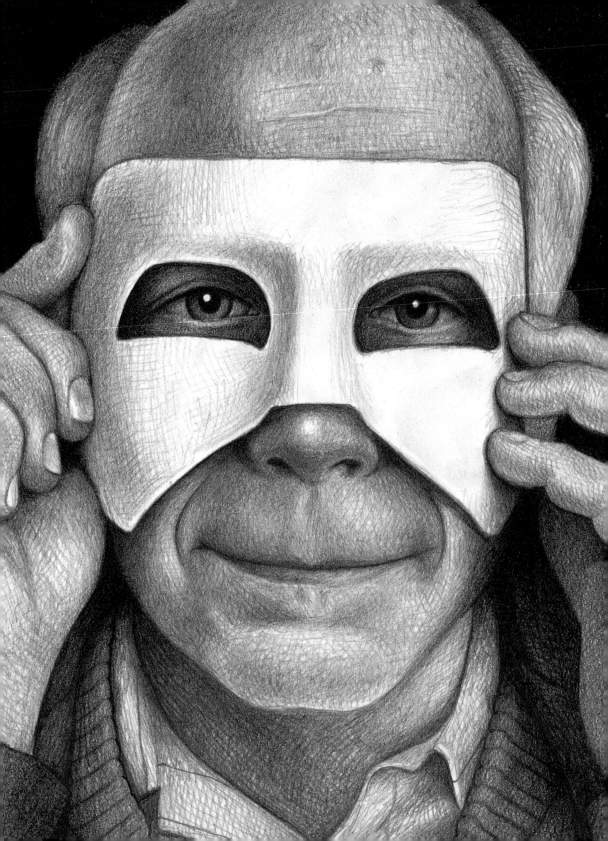

"Mr. Shadows is dead," I whispered.

"He *was* dead, Alonzo. You brought him back to life! I made those programs years ago because I loved monsters, just like you. But they took my show off the air, and that was the end of Mr. Shadows. My father got me a job delivering mail, and I vowed to forget about *Monsters at Midnight.* So imagine my surprise, all these years later, when I found your letter at the post office! That's why I started telling the stories about The Beast. Now *everyone* believes in monsters!"

"But I'm not The Beast," I cried. "I'm just a boy, and no one will believe me!"

"You're not just a boy," said Mr. Blake. "You are The Boy of a Thousand Faces!"

"I'm *not*," I said. "I'm not even close."

Mr. Blake slipped the white mask over my face. Then he made me a cape out of a bedsheet and said, "You're going to be late for school, Alonzo."

My birthday was a blur of cupcakes and costumes. After school we all swarmed outside and went trick-or-treating for so long that we were still ringing doorbells as it grew dark. Eventually I headed back to my apartment building. My footsteps echoed as I neared the door. Suddenly the quiet was shattered by the sound of classical music. I spun around. A white rectangle of light appeared on the side of the building across the street, and to my amazement a movie began.

It was *The Phantom of the Opera*.

People heard the music or saw the light, and a crowd gathered to watch the movie. I snuck away and climbed up to the roof of my apartment building. There I found Mr. Blake running an old-fashioned film projector and a boom box.

He smiled when he saw me, and we sat down at the edge of our roof and watched our favorite movie together, under the Halloween stars.

When it was over, everyone who had gathered below looked up to see who had shown them this incredible movie. Mr. Blake reached from behind me and removed my glittering white mask. The crowd cheered.

We climbed down from the roof and were swallowed up by all the costumed kids. We were reflected in the glassy red eyes of a thousand masks and made-up faces. Every single kid was dressed as their version of The Beast, and The Beast was *me*! Here at last were my thousand faces.

Mr. Blake put his coat around my shoulders, and slowly the monsters went home. My mom met us at the apartment door and gave me my birthday present. It was a brand-new Polaroid camera.

All across town we shed our masks and costumes, washed the makeup away, and put aside our plastic fangs. House by house The Beast was laid to rest for the evening, some in piles on the floor and some tucked carefully into drawers.

Alone in my room, as Halloween ended, I picked up my new camera and took one last picture of myself. Carefully, I taped it into my monster notebook, and below it I proudly wrote what I had always wanted to write . . .

Alonzo King The Boy of a Thousand
Faces age 11

32 USA
Lon Chaney as
THE PHANTOM OF THE OPERA
1997
32 USA
Bela Lugosi as
DRACULA
1997
32 USA
Boris Karloff in
FRANKENSTEIN
1997
32 USA
Boris Karloff as
The MUMMY
1997
32 USA
Lon Chaney, Jr. as
THE WOLF MAN
1997
32 USA
Lon Chaney as
THE PHANTOM OF THE OPERA
1997
32 USA
Bela Lugosi as
DRACULA
1997
32 USA
Boris Karloff in
FRANKENSTEIN
1997
32 USA
Boris Karloff as
The MUMMY
1997
32 USA
Lon Chaney, Jr. as
THE WOLF MAN
1997
32 USA
Lon Chaney as
THE PHANTOM OF THE OPERA
1997
32 USA
Bela Lugosi as
DRACULA
1997
32 USA
Boris Karloff in
FRANKENSTEIN
1997
32 USA
Boris Karloff as
The MUMMY
1997
32 USA
Lon Chaney, Jr. as
THE WOLF MAN
1997
32 USA
Lon Chaney as
THE PHANTOM OF THE OPERA
1997
32 USA
Bela Lugosi as
DRACULA
1997
32 USA
Boris Karloff in
FRANKENSTEIN
1997
32 USA
Boris Karloff as
The MUMMY
1997
32 USA
Lon Chaney, Jr. as
THE WOLF MAN
1997
32 USA
Lon Chaney as
THE PHANTOM OF THE OPERA
1997
32 USA
Bela Lugosi as
DRACULA
1997
32 USA
Boris Karloff in
FRANKENSTEIN
1997
32 USA
Boris Karloff as
The MUMMY
1997
32 USA
Lon Chaney, Jr. as
THE WOLF MAN
1997
32 USA
Lon Chaney as
THE PHANTOM OF THE OPERA
1997
32 USA
Bela Lugosi as
DRACULA
1997
32 USA
Boris Karloff in
FRANKENSTEIN
1997
32 USA
Lon Chaney as
THE PHANTOM OF THE OPERA
1997
32 USA
Bela Lugosi as
DRACULA
1997
32 USA
Boris Karloff in
FRANKENSTEIN
1997
32 USA
Boris Karloff as
The MUMMY
1997
32 USA
Lon Chaney, Jr. as
THE WOLF MAN
1997
32 USA
Lon Chaney as
THE PHANTOM OF THE OPERA
1997
32 USA
Bela Lugosi as
DRACULA
1997
32 USA
Boris Karloff in
FRANKENSTEIN
1997
32 USA
Boris Karloff as
The MUMMY
1997
32 USA
Lon Chaney, Jr. as
THE WOLF MAN
1997
32 USA
Lon Chaney as
THE PHANTOM OF THE OPERA
1997
32 USA
Bela Lugosi as
DRACULA
1997
32 USA
Boris Karloff in
FRANKENSTEIN
1997
32 USA
Boris Karloff as
The MUMMY
1997
32 USA
Lon Chaney, Jr. as
THE WOLF MAN
1997
32 USA
Lon Chaney as
THE PHANTOM OF THE OPERA
1997
32 USA
Bela Lugosi as
DRACULA
1997
32 USA
Boris Karloff in
FRANKENSTEIN
1997
32 USA
Boris Karloff as
The MUMMY
1997
32 USA
Lon Chaney, Jr. as
THE WOLF MAN
1997
32 USA
Lon Chaney as
THE PHANTOM OF THE OPERA
1997